# Master Track's Train

# Ahlberg & Amstutz

**PUFFIN**

PUFFIN BOOKS

UK | USA | Canada | Ireland | Australia
India | New Zealand | South Africa

Puffin Books is part of the Penguin Random House group of companies
whose addresses can be found at global.penguinrandomhouse.com.

www.penguin.co.uk    www.puffin.co.uk    www.ladybird.co.uk

First published in hardback by Viking and in paperback by Puffin Books 1997
This edition published 2017

001

Text copyright © Allan Ahlberg, 1997
Illustrations copyright © André Amstutz, 1997
Educational Advisory Editor: Brian Thompson

Printed in China
A CIP catalogue record for this book is available from the British Library

ISBN: 978-0-723-29393-4

All correspondence to:
Puffin Books, Penguin Random House Children's
80 Strand, London WC2R 0RL

# HERE IS AN ANNOUNCEMENT:

The train approaching platform two
is full of stolen goods,
crowded with crooks
and a day and a half late.

British Rail are sorry for the delay.

How could this happen? you ask.
Well, listen and I'll tell you . . .
all about it.

The story began many years ago,
with a little train,
a big driver,
a big driver's wife,
an empty platform
and a handbag.

Yes – a handbag.

Mr Track (he was the driver)
picked up the bag.
Mrs Track (she was the driver's wife)
peeped inside.
And what did they find?

A *baby*.

Mr and Mrs Track took the baby
to the Lost Property Office.
When no one claimed him,
they took him home
to live with them.

LOST PROPERTY

"We will call him . . . Toby," they said.
And they did.

Toby Track was a good baby,
a good toddler
(well, nearly),
a good little boy
and a good big boy.

He went everywhere
with his mum and dad.

As he got older,
he helped with the tickets,
the sandwiches
and lots of other jobs.

Then, one morning,
just two days ago,
a terrible thing happened.

Mr and Mrs Track woke up to find
that Toby's bed was empty
and the train had gone.

Help! you say.
How could this
happen?
Well, listen . . .
and you'll hear.

Toby Track had woken in the night
to find:

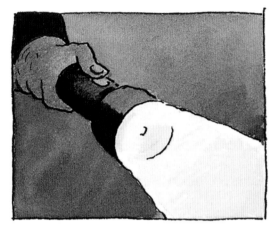

a shining torch,

a whispering voice,

a grabbing hand,

running feet

and a *moving* train.

The *stolen* train puffed off into the night.

On board, a *family* of crooks:

bad dad,      bad mum,

two bad children
and a bad dog.

Their name was CREEP!

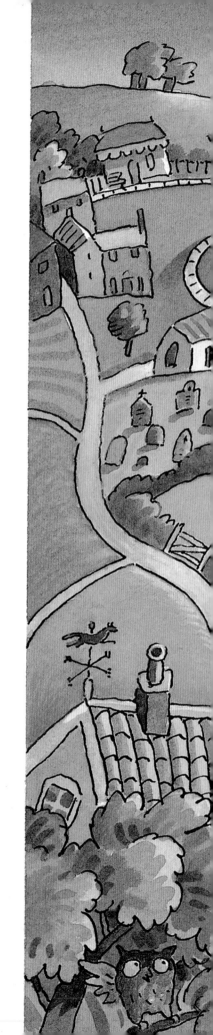

The train puffed on.
It stopped
and started
and stopped
and started.

The Creeps were stealing
as they went along:
anything and everything,
this – that – and the other.

They worked all night.
When morning came they hid . . .

in a tunnel.

The Creeps sat in the guard's van
and ate their stolen breakfasts.

Then, worn out and pleased
with themselves, they fell asleep.

Out crept Toby Track.

Yes, out crept Toby.
He knew how to lock the guard's van,
so he locked it.
He knew how to drive the train,
so he drove it.
He didn't know his way home,
so he got lost . . .

for a while.

But what about the Creeps? you ask.
Well, they yelled and they banged,
but they couldn't get out
of the van.
See . . .
here comes the train now
and they're still in it!

And here comes Toby!

And here come Mr and Mrs Track,
who are just so pleased to see him.

Yes, a happy ending,
except that . . .
wait a minute . . .

HERE IS ANOTHER
ANNOUNCEMENT:

The train approaching
platforms four, five and six
is coming in sideways.
What a disaster!
How could this happen? you ask.

"No!"
"No more announcements."
"It's late!"
"And, anyway, we must go now –

"We've got a train to catch!"